PROGRAMMED
FOR LAUGHS

A Robot Joke Book

By Matt Chapman
Illustrated by Lily Nishita

This book is a work of fiction. Any references to historical events, real people, or real places are used fictitiously. Other names, characters, places, and events are products of the author's imagination, and any resemblance to actual events or places or persons, living or dead, is entirely coincidental.

SIMON SPOTLIGHT

An imprint of Simon & Schuster Children's Publishing Division

1230 Avenue of the Americas, New York, New York 10020

This Simon Spotlight edition September 2020

TM & © 2020 Sony Pictures Animation Inc. All Rights Reserved.

All rights reserved, including the right of reproduction in whole or in part in any form.

SIMON SPOTLIGHT and colophon are registered trademarks of Simon & Schuster, Inc.

For information about special discounts for bulk purchases, please contact Simon & Schuster Special Sales at 1-866-506-1949 or business@simonandschuster.com.

The text of this book was set in Bluberry.

Manufactured in the United States of America 0720 OFF

2 4 6 8 10 9 7 5 3 1

ISBN 978-1-5344-7810-7

ISBN 978-1-5344-7811-4 (eBook)

CONTENTS

TAKE ME TO YOUR LEADER!
ROBOT JOKES

Why were the baby robots crying?
They missed their mama and data.

Why are Deborahbot 5000 and Eric so good at tennis?
They are programmed to serve.

What is a robot's favorite kind of music?
Heavy metal!

Why was the robot so sad at summer camp?
He missed his father and motherboard.

Knock, knock!
Who's there?
Robots.
Robots who?
WE ASK THE QUESTIONS NOW, HUMAN!

Why couldn't the robot catch any butterflies?
He couldn't seem to make the network.

How did the robot graduate from school so fast?
It kept getting upgraded.

Why was the baby robot alone with its mama?
Because its data was missing.

Why did the robot have to go back to school?
Because its skills were getting a little rusty!

Why did the robot go to the doctor?
Because it had a virus!

What's a robot's favorite dance?
Doing "The Human."

How does a robot spider capture an entire planet?
With a world wide web.

What's a robot spider's favorite meal?
Programming bugs.

What do robot spiders do once they've caught their prey?
They upload them to their website.

How do robot spiders take their family pictures?
With their webcam.

Why did the robot keep going to the dentist?
Because of its Bluetooth.

What's a robot's favorite thing to order at a Mexican restaurant?
Microchips and salsa.

Why was Deborahbot 5000 mad?
People kept pushing her buttons!

What did the robot do when it was sick to its stomach?
It uploaded its lunch.

Did you hear about the robot that lost its shoes?
It had to reboot!

How does a robot's body fight off computer viruses?
With white blood cellphones.

That's a big slice of FUNNY!

What pests do robot dogs hate the most?
Robofleas and robo-ticks.

Who is a robot's favorite author?
Anne Droid!

What did the robot coach say to give its team a pep talk?
"You all need to get with the programmers!"

Why should you tell robots all your secrets?
Because they will keep them on the download.

Why did Eric and Deborahbot 5000 have trouble
communicating with each other?
They got their wires crossed.

Why couldn't the little robot ride the roller coaster?
He was too short-circuited.

How do robots roast marshmallows?
Over a Wi-Fire.

What did the doctor tell the robot about its diet?
"Be sure you eat plenty of Wi-Fiber."

What did the robot do when it felt sick at the smartphone store?
It took a tablet.

Why did Eric and Deborahbot 5000 sit on the couch all Saturday and Sunday?
On the weekends, they like to unplug.

What kind of salad do robots like?
Anything with ice-borg lettuce!

Why did the robot throw itself in the lake?
It was using arti-fish-al intelligence.

Why did the robot take its girlfriend out to dinner in a hot-air balloon?
It was trying to update.

How do robots seal a business deal?
With a firmware handshake.

What do you get when you cross a robot and a squid?
Artificial ink-telligence.

ROTFL!

How do soccer robots keep cool during games?
They stand near the fans!

What advice did the robot students get at graduation?
"Remember, life is full of uploads and downloads."

What do you get when you cross a robot and a fairy-tale monster?
Version 2.0gre.

What do robot families like doing together?
Playing circuit-board games.

Why was the robot so tiny?
It was an ant-droid.

Why were the robots playing music?
They were band-droids.

Why were the robots following the Internet celebrity?
They were fan-droids.

What do you call a robot architect?
A plan-droid.

Why wouldn't the robots go in the water?
They were land-droids.

Why didn't the robot ever use salt or pepper on its food?
It was a bland-droid.

What do you call a solar-powered robot at the beach?
A tan-droid.

What kind of robot really believes in itself?
A yes-I-candroid.

That's FUNNY!

What do you call a robot's father's father's father?
His great-grand-droid.

What do you call a robot that tells too many robot jokes?
An I-can't-stand-droid!

What do you call a robot that only goes out in winter?
A snowbot!

What's the best kind of robot to have with you in the dark?
A glowbot!

What do you call a robot that can't make up its mind?
A yes-and-nobot.

Why did the humans aid the robots instead of fighting them?
Because they were pro-bot.

That was a GOOD ONE!

What do you call a robot that doesn't wear shoes?
A toe-bot.

What do you call someone dressed up like a robot?
A faux-bot.

What do you call a vanishing robot?
A where-did-you-go-bot!

What did the cashier say when the robot asked for new batteries?
"Okay, but I'll have to charge you."

Why did the robots sneak into the zoo when their batteries were running low?
So the rhinos could charge them.

Why was the robot bankrupt?
He had used all his cache!

What happened to the robot that was climbing a tree?
He logged off.

What do robots love to play on guitar?
Power chords!

Where does robot honey come from?
From USBees!

How are baby robots born?
They're delivered by drones.

Why did the robot tell such boring stories?
Because it was a drone.

Why did the robot have to go to the bathroom?
Because its inbox was full.

What did the robot say when someone asked if it had to use the restroom?

"Error. Does not com-poot."

How do robots drive a car?

They put their metal to the pedal!

"Does not COM-POOT!" That's funny!

What do you call the search for bugs in a robot's system?
A glitch hunt.

How does a bugbite make a robot feel?
Glitchy!

What do Eric and Deborahbot 5000 do when they're hungry?
They eat a megabyte!

TECHNOLOGY JOKES

Why are computers so bad at football?
They're always running out of ram.

Why was the computer in a bad mood when it came home from work?
Because it had a hard drive home.

Why is it so easy for computers to get out of jail?
They just press escape.

HA, HA, HA!

How did the computer win the hot-dog-eating contest?
It took megabytes.

Why was the PAL personal assistant looking for her files on an airplane?
Because they were in the cloud.

What's a computer's favorite breakfast cereal?
Ones and Zeerios.

How do computers make s'mores?
They use pro-graham crackers.

Why couldn't the computer remember its password?
It was low on memory.

Why couldn't the Internet browser pay for its meal?
It had just cleared its cache.

Why did the PAL Labs employee start dancing in front of her mom instead of building computers like she was supposed to?
Because she didn't want to make her motherboard.

What comes right before video chat?
Video chit.

What do you call a computer's favorite pants?
Browser trousers.

What's a smartphone's favorite part of a meal?
The apps.

Why did the computer squeak?
Because someone stepped on its mouse!

What's a smartphone's favorite kind of restaurant?
Text-Mex.

"Stepped on its mouse!"

BWHA, HA, HA!

Why did the smartphone get so sick?
It caught a viral video.

How did the smartphone propose to its girlfriend?
With an engagement ringtone.

What's a pirate's favorite gadget?
A smAARRRtphone.

What kind of clothing do computers put on to get comfy?
Their softwear.

What do you get when you cross a computer and a lifeguard?
A screensaver!

Did you hear about the burglar who stole 100 touch screens?
He swiped them all.

HA, HA, HA, HA!

Who do computers visit during the holidays?
Their programaws and programpaws.

How did the computer pay for its groceries?
It wrote a systems check.

How does a website like its eggs cooked?
Sunny-side upload.

"Sunny-side upload!"
Egg-shellent joke!

What does a proud computer call its child?
A microchip off the old block!

Why was the smartphone so impatient at the restaurant?
Because it wasn't getting any service!

Why did the smartphone enjoy the wedding so much?
Because it had a good reception.

How did the detective solve the mystery of the broken smartphone?
He cracked the case!

How does an audience show its appreciation for a website?
They give it a round of uploads.

What's a computer's favorite kind of ice cream?
Softserveware.

Why did the computer put itself in the freezer?
It wanted to turn its software into hardware.

Why did the smart speaker start playing cards?
Because its owner set it to shuffle.

"Do you know if this coffee shop has good wireless Internet?"
"I heard it's Wi-Fine."

SO FUNNY!

What do you call someone's personal wireless Internet?
My-Fi.

What do you call a store's wireless Internet?
Buy-Fi.

What do you call a graveyard's wireless Internet?
Die-Fi.

Why can't computers play tennis?
They're always trying to surf the 'net!

What do you call a secret agent's wireless Internet?
Spy-Fi.

What do you call a bakery's wireless Internet?
Pie-Fi.

What does a baby computer call its father?
Data!

What do you call a French poodle's wireless Internet?
Fi-Fi.

What do you say when you've heard too many wireless Internet jokes?
"WHY, OH WHY?!-Fi!"

What do you get when you cross a computer with an elephant?

Lots of memory!

Now that humans have invented A.I., what comes next?

B.I., C.I., D.I., E.I., F.I. . . .

What does a computer do before it goes hiking?

It boots up!

ROFL!

Did you hear about the website that went on a terrible vacation?
It couldn't wait to get homepage.

Why did the computer get glasses?
To improve its website!

BWHA, HA, HA!

Did you hear about the sad website?
It's been down all day.

Why did the lonely kid keep taking people's headphones?
She was hoping to find an earbud.

How did the smartphone get upstairs by itself?
It used its GPScalator.

Another
slice of
FUNNY!

What does a smartphone do when it needs to wake up really fast?
It drinks a GPSpresso.

Why do driverless vehicles make such good getaway cars?
They always make their GPScape.

Why did it keep raining on the computer programmer?
She was doing some cloud computing.

Why was the computer so angry?
It had a chip on its shoulder!

What do you call an Internet comedian?
A stand-upload comic.

Why did the cat sit on the keyboard?
To keep an eye on the mouse!

What happened when the two computers met?
It was love at first site!

Where do emails stay when they're on vacation?
An innbox.

Why did the website go to the spa?
It needed to be refreshed.

BWHA, HA, HA, HA, HA!

Why did the smartphone think its first date went well?
It got good signals.

Why shouldn't you trust spiders?
They post stuff on the web!

HA, HA, HA!

Why didn't the power cord want to be plugged in?
Because it was a-frayed.

What did the dentist say to the computer?
"Don't worry. This won't hurt a byte!"

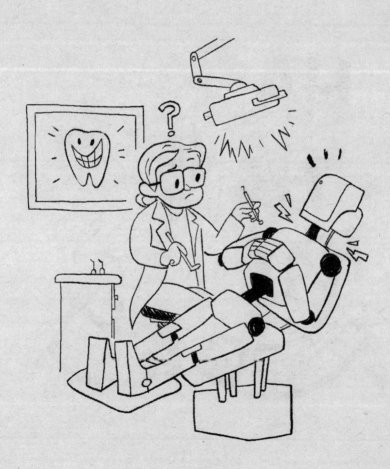

What did one keyboard say to the other?

"You're just my type!"

Why was the website so selfish?

Because it was a social ME-dia site, not a social YOU-dia site.

What was taking the computer so long?
It kept inSTALLing.

How did the tree get on the Internet?
It logged on!

LOL!

What vitamin do computers need most?
Vitamin USB$_{12}$.

Why are cats so good at video games?
Because they have nine lives!

What do you say when you lose a video game?
"I want a Wii-match!"

Why are fish so into online gaming?
They love all the streaming.

Did you hear about the kid who played online
games while kayaking?
He streamed the whole thing!

Why did the gamer keep doing somersaults?
They were playing a roll-playing game.

Why does Aaron always sit on the roof when he and Katie play video games?
So he can get a higher score than her.

HA, HA, HA, HA!

What's a pirate's favorite type of video game?
V-Aarrr!

"Is your Xbox running?"
"Yes, why?"
"You'd better catch it before it runs out the door!"

That's a GOOD one!

"Get a life!"

"Ha! I'm a gamer—I've got plenty of lives!"

Before esports, what kind of sports were there?
Dsports, csports, bsports, and asports.

That's a big slice of FUNNY!

Knock, knock!
Who's there?
Nacho!
Nacho who?
Nacho game, Pepper, play something else!

What's a gamer's favorite drink?
Virtual Reali-TEA.

Knock, knock!
Who's there?
Wii.
Wii who?
I want a Wii-match!

HA! HA! HA! HA!

BECAUSE I SAID SO!

PARENT JOKES

Why did Mr. Mitchell tuck his phone into bed?
Mrs. Mitchell told him to put it in sleep mode.

Why did the Mitchells invite Aaron's crush over for a BBQ?
So she could be grilled!

LOL!!!

Why did Aaron bring two insects to school?
Because he heard it was Pair-Ants Night.

Knock, knock!
Who's there?
Lena.
Lena who?
Lena a little closer so Mama can give you a kiss!

Why did Mrs. Mitchell put their family photos in a cage?
She wanted to capture the memories.

What kind of bread are kids always giving their parents?
Eye rolls.

Why did Mr. Mitchell superglue everyone to their chairs at the dinner table?
He wanted some family bonding time.

What's the difference between a baby and a dog?
One will poop all the time, chew up your pillows, and slobber all over everything. The other one is a dog.

What did the baby corn say to the mama corn?
"Where is the pop corn?"

Why don't kids like to see their parents kissing?
Because it's gross. Please stop talking about it.

Why wouldn't Mrs. Mitchell let Aaron watch viral videos?
She said they were a bad influenza on him.

ARE WE THERE YET?

ROAD TRIP JOKES

The Mitchells stopped for gas, but they never left. Why?
Because they were at a gas stay-tion, not a gas leave-tion!

Why didn't Katie want to use the restroom when the Mitchells stopped on their road trip?
Because it was a gross-ery store.

LOL!

Katie: What do follicles ask their parents on long car rides?
Aaron: Are we hair yet?

Aaron: What do cubs ask their parents on long car rides?
Katie: Are we bears yet?

Katie: What do French pastries ask their parents on long car rides?

Aaron: Are weclair yet?

Aaron: What do planes ask their parents on long flights?

Katie: Are we there, jet?

What game do smartphones play in the car on road trips?

I Spy Wi-Fi.

HA, HA, HA!

Who is your family friend that comes on every long road trip?
Bill Board.

Did you hear about the twenty-two-wheeler that drove across the country?
It was really TIRE-d!

LOL! LOL! LOL!

Why did Aaron think Mr. Mitchell was being selfish on their road trip?
He kept talking about mi-leage but didn't care at all about your-leage!

Where did the chicken want to go?
Just to the next egg-sit.

Why did Aaron throw the motel's pancakes and eggs out the window?
Because a sign told him to FREE BREAKFAST!

How do you calculate where the next rest area will be on a road trip?
Rest Length x Rest Width = Rest Area.

Why did Aaron ignore all the scenic views when his family would stop at them?

Because the signs kept telling him to OVERLOOK!

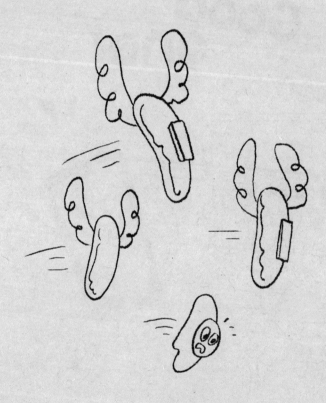

What do you call a potato family's vacation?
A road chip!

OH, BROTHER!

SIBLING JOKES

Aaron: Why did the velociraptor stop running?

Katie: I dunno, why?

Aaron: Because it had dino-SORE feet!

Aaron: What did one T. rex say to the other after they robbed a bank?

Katie: I have no idea.

Aaron: Do you think anyone SAURUS?

Aaron: What do IDK, LY, and TTYL mean?

Katie: I don't know. Love you. Talk to you later.

Aaron: Okay, I'll ask Mom!

Katie: Aaron, why did you cut a hole in my new umbrella?

Aaron: So you could tell when it stopped raining!

How are teenage siblings like history museums?
They're quiet, creepy, and if you touch their stuff, they freak out!

Why was Aaron searching the house with a magnifying glass?
Because Katie told him to "Get a clue."

Why did Aaron give Katie a big stack of cash?
Because she was always saying, "Leave me a loan."

Have you ever been camping with your siblings?
It can be in tents!

What did the little tree say to its older sister?
"Us siblings gotta *stick* together!"

Why were the brother and sister lumberjacks always fighting?
They just couldn't get a log.

That was SO FUNNY!

DOGGONE FUNNY!

DOG JOKES

Why doesn't Aaron like playing video games with Monchi?

Because Monchi keeps pressing paws.

How do tech-savvy dogs keep in touch with friends?
They text one another on their smartbones.

That's a big slice of
FUNNY!

How do tech-savvy dogs keep their smartbones working?

They get the latest software pupdates.

Why does Monchi like to watch Aaron play adventure games?

He likes all the fetch quests.

How do you clean up after a robotic dog?
Just click un-doo!

"Un-doo!"
Get it?!
Ha, ha!

How do robotic dogs know where to go to the bathroom?
They have built-in GPeeS.

What's Monchi's favorite kind of video game?
Vir-chew-al reality.

BWHA, HA, HA!

Did you hear about the dog who worked at the butcher shop?
I hear he really ate his job.

What's black and white and slobbers uncontrollably?
Monchi in a tuxedo!

What's black and white and slobbers uncontrollably
and zooms through the ocean?
Monchi in a tuxedo on a torpedo!

What's black and white and slobbers uncontrollably and zooms through the ocean and smells like beans and rice?
Monchi in a tuxedo on a torpedo with a burrito!